The
W★itch
Next Door

Maverick
Chapter Readers

'The Witch Next Door'
An original concept by Jenny Jinks
© Jenny Jinks

Illustrated by Amy Lane

Published by MAVERICK ARTS PUBLISHING LTD

Studio 11, City Business Centre, 6 Brighton Road,

Horsham, West Sussex, RH13 5BB

© Maverick Arts Publishing Limited August 2021

+44 (0)1403 256941

A CIP catalogue record for this book is available at the British Library.

ISBN 978-1-84886-800-7

www.maverickbooks.co.uk

This book is rated as: Lime Band (Guided Reading)

The Witch Next Door

Written by
Jenny Jinks

Illustrated by
Amy Lane

Chapter 1

"Catch this!" Ollie shouted.

The ball whizzed way out of Beth's reach, and got stuck in a tree.

Beth could hear Ollie laughing as she scrambled up the tree to fetch it. She could see right into next-door's garden from up there. Beth shuddered. She was sure the old lady who lived there was really a witch. If only she could prove it.

She dragged her eyes away from the creepy house, grabbed the ball, and jumped to the ground.

Right, thought Beth. *Let's see him catch this.*

Beth threw the ball as hard as she could. It spun right past Ollie, and straight through the open kitchen window.

CRASH!

Beth and Ollie rushed inside. Mum's favourite vase lay smashed on the floor.

"Oh no," Beth moaned.

"Maybe she won't notice it's missing?" Ollie said. "Quick, let's clean it up!"

They hunted for a broom, but couldn't find one anywhere.

"How can your mum not own a broom? She's the neatest person ever!" Ollie said.

Beth shrugged. It was true, Mum kept the house spotless. They must have a broom somewhere.

Beth remembered seeing a broom propped against the house next door. It would be okay if they borrowed it, wouldn't it…?

"Are you kidding?" Ollie screeched when she told him her plan. "You want to *steal* from a *witch!* She'll probably curse you and turn your skin purple!"

"It's only borrowing," Beth pointed out. But Ollie still refused to come.

So Beth headed next door, alone.

Chapter 2

Beth looked at the old, run-down house. She knew she should ring the bell and ask to borrow the broom. But she really didn't want to, and it didn't look like anyone was home. Besides, she would return it before anyone even knew it was gone.

Beth crept round to the side gate. It opened with an eerie **CREAK!**

There was the broom, leaning against the house.

Beth went to grab it. But as soon as she grabbed the broom she started to feel strange. Her hands felt warm and tingly. And before she knew what was happening…

Beth was swept right off her feet. The broom floated up... up... up into the air, and it was taking her with it!

Beth dangled dangerously below the broom; her eyes squeezed shut as it wobbled about. Beth gripped the handle tightly, but somehow she knew she wasn't going to fall. It was like the broom was stuck to her hands.

Finally it stopped. It felt like the broom was waiting for instructions.

"I want to get down," Beth said.

The broom slowly lowered her back down. Beth felt the bond between her hands and the broomstick break, and she dropped to the ground. The broom fell back against the wall, looking like it had never moved.

"Whoa," Beth sighed. "That was magic!"

Chapter 3

"What do I do?" Ollie asked. Beth had dragged him straight round to the witch's house next door. She had babbled about a flying broomstick. But it just looked like an ordinary broom to him.

"Pick it up!" said Beth.

Ollie picked up the broom.

"Well..." Beth bobbed up and down excitedly.

"It's not doing anything," Ollie said.

"Do your hands feel weird?"

Ollie shook his head. "Maybe you imagined it?"

"I didn't! It flew, I promise," Beth said. "You're just doing it wrong. Give it here."

Beth was about to grab the broom when a loud honking outside made them both jump. Ollie's dad had arrived.

"We'd better get out of here," Ollie said.

"But..." Beth began. She gave one last longing look at the broomstick, before creeping after Ollie.

Chapter 4

Before Ollie left, he made Beth promise not to go next door again without him.

Beth tried to stay away, but she was desperate to know more about the witch. And she couldn't wait to have another go on that broom! So, barely five minutes later, Beth was letting herself back through the side gate.

The broomstick was gone.

The old witch must be home! Beth knew she should go straight home and wait to come back with Ollie. But it couldn't hurt to have a quick peek around the garden first.

To Beth's disappointment, it was just like a normal garden—just a bit overgrown. Then Beth spotted an old shed. It was broken, dark and almost entirely hidden by ivy—the perfect place to keep secrets.

Beth tried the door. But, even though it looked like a sneeze could blow it down, the door didn't budge.

Beth was ready to give up when she spotted something down the side of the shed.

The broom!

Beth couldn't help herself. She reached out and grabbed it. The tingling feeling spread through her. But this time she was ready. She sat on the broom as it floated upwards. It felt like she had been riding a broom her whole life as she whizzed around the witch's garden. She could have stayed up there forever.

Finally she brought the broomstick down to land. She was just tucking it safely back beside the shed when she heard the **creeeeaaaak** of the side gate, and the sound of shuffling footsteps.

The witch was coming.

Chapter 5

Beth had to hide, and fast. She could hear the footsteps getting closer. She tried the shed handle again, but still it didn't budge.

Please open, she pleaded.

There was a strange tingling in her hands, a click, and suddenly the shed door sprung open.

Beth darted inside and shut the door behind her, just in time. Then she waited. She listened to the old lady pottering around the garden. Finally the back door slammed, and the lady was gone.

Beth ran straight home. She shut herself in her bedroom. Her mind was racing. How had the shed door suddenly unlocked? Why did the broom work for her, but not for Ollie? Maybe the broom was cursed. Had it passed its magic on to her? She had to find out. She locked her bedroom door. Then she thought about unlocking it, just as she had with the shed.

CLICK!

It worked! Her door unlocked.

Beth couldn't believe it. Somehow, she had

got actual magic powers!

Chapter 6

Beth spent ages exploring what her new powers could do. She moved a stack of books across her room and opened her drawers, all without touching them!

The front door slammed downstairs. Mum was home.

The vase! Beth had completely forgotten to clear it up. She rushed downstairs to explain. Mum was not happy when Beth showed her the broken vase, but it was when Beth told her about going next door that Mum got really mad.

"Did you touch anything?" Mum said.

"I was only going to borrow the broom," Beth explained. "Why don't we have one?"

"Do you have any idea how dangerous that was? If you had..." Mum stopped and took a deep breath. "You must never do that again, do you

understand? Go up to your room. At least you can't get into any more trouble there."

Beth stormed off up to her room.

Why was Mum so cross? Was she hiding something? Did she already know about the witch? Beth wished she could talk to Ollie. He always knew just what to do. But there was no way Mum would let her go out now. It would have to wait. Until then, she had plenty of time to have fun with her new powers!

Chapter 7

First thing the next morning, Beth raced round to Ollie's house.

"I have so much to tell you," Beth said in a rush, before Ollie could even say hello. Beth told him everything about her trip next door, how she rode the broom again, nearly getting caught and her mum's strange reaction.

"We finally have proof! Next-door is definitely, absolutely, one hundred percent a witch! And I think Mum already knows!"

Beth waited for Ollie to say something. He had a strange expression on his face.

"You went back without me?" he said slowly.

"We can go again. Let's go now."

"Why? So you can pretend there's a magic broomstick again? Strange how it only works when I'm not there, isn't it."

Beth stared at Ollie. "You don't believe me? Come on, I'll show you. I'm sure the broom will work for you this time."

Ollie didn't say anything. He just looked at his feet.

"I think you should leave," he said.

Beth couldn't believe it. How could her best friend not believe her?! She hadn't even had a chance to tell him about her powers. She turned and ran before Ollie could see the tears streaming down her face.

Chapter 8

When Beth got home, Mum was sitting at the kitchen table.

"What's wrong?" Mum asked.

The whole story exploded out of Beth in one big jumble of words. Mum sat quietly and listened. Beth expected her to be cross again. But she just looked sad.

"I'm sorry," Mum finally said.

"I don't understand," Beth said. "Why doesn't Ollie believe me? And why did you get so cross? It feels like you're keeping something from me."

"You're right. I have been keeping something from you," Mum said slowly. "Perhaps I should have told you a long time ago. I was just trying to protect you."

"The truth is..." said Mum. Beth held her breath. This was it. Mum was finally going to tell her what she had known for ages—that her neighbour was a real-life witch. "The truth is, you're a witch."

Chapter 9

"I knew it!" cried Beth. And then she stopped.

"Wait, what? You mean our *neighbour's* a witch."

"No, Beth. You are. We are. We're witches."

Mum pointed to her mug.

It floated off the table.

Beth stared at her mum in disbelief.

"I was going to tell you, when you were ready. Until then, I just had to keep you away

from anything that might activate your powers—broomsticks, black cats and such. I made sure we never had them in the house. I had to keep you away from it."

"But why?" Beth asked.

"I always knew I was magic. When I told my friends, they all treated me differently. Some thought I was making it up. Others were scared of me because I was different. I was very lonely, Beth. I didn't want that to happen to you."

"Ollie would never do that to me," Beth said.

Mum shrugged. "I hope you're right."

Mum wasn't right... was she?

Beth started to feel worried. Ollie already didn't believe her about the broomstick. What if he didn't believe this either? Or worse... what if he was scared of her? Beth had been scared of the witch next door. Is that how people would think of her now? Would Ollie even still want to be friends?

Chapter 10

Beth sat in her room, thinking everything through. She couldn't believe she was a witch. And she couldn't imagine keeping something like that from her best friend. They told each other everything. But she didn't want to scare him away.

A while later, there was a gentle tap on her door. Ollie's face peered round it.

"Your mum let me in," he said. "I'm really sorry about before. I just felt really left out. Your neighbour is a witch, and you got to ride a broomstick. All the exciting things always happen to you."

Beth laughed nervously. If only he knew!

"Do you want to go and see if we can find any more magic stuff now?" Ollie asked.

Beth looked at Ollie. He did believe her after all. And he didn't look scared at the thought of a witch, he looked... excited.

"I know something better we can do," Beth smiled. "I've got something to show you."

Beth looked at the pillow next to Ollie. Suddenly it lifted up, then dropped on Ollie's head. Ollie turned white. He stared at Beth, his eyes wide.

Beth began to panic. What if she had scared Ollie off?

But Ollie couldn't hold it in any longer.

"You're *magic?!*" he burst out. Beth nodded.

"That's so cool! What else can you do?"

"I'll show you. But first we have something very important to do," Beth said. "How do you fancy flying on a broomstick?"

Ollie looked like he might burst with excitement.

Beth beamed at him. She was sure her life would be very different from now on. But one thing would never change. She would always have her best friend.

Discussion Points

1. Why did Beth have to go find a broom in the beginning?

2. What happened when Beth found out the shed was locked?

a) The witch next door found her

b) She unlocked it with magic

c) She found the key to open it

3. What was your favourite part of the story?

4. Who makes the broom fly?

5. Why do you think Beth's mum didn't tell her they were witches?

6. Who was your favourite character and why?

7. There were moments in the story when Beth had to **investigate**. Where do you think the story shows this most?

8. What do you think happens after the end of the story?

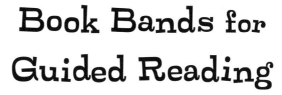

Book Bands for Guided Reading

The Institute of Education book banding system is a scale of colours that reflects the various levels of reading difficulty. The bands are assigned by taking into account the content, the language style, the layout and phonics. Word, phrase and sentence level work is also taken into consideration.

The Maverick Readers Scheme is a bright, attractive range of books covering the pink to grey bands. All of these books have been book banded for guided reading to the industry standard and edited by a leading educational consultant.

To view the whole Maverick Readers scheme, visit our website at

www.maverickearlyreaders.com

Or scan the QR code to view our scheme instantly!

Maverick Chapter Readers

(From Lime to Grey Band)

Pink
Red
Yellow
Blue
Green
Orange
Turquoise
Purple
Gold
White
Lime
Brown
Grey